GRAPHIC NOVELS

STONE ARCH BOOKS
a capstone imprint

UP NEXT)))

on **Sports Illustrated KIDS**

TRACK TEAM TITANS

FOLLOWED BY:

TITANS ANNOUNCE TRACK AND FIELD TEAM SIGNUPS BEGINN

SCHOOL'S TOP ATHLETES TO TRY OUT FOR TITANS' TRACK TEAM!

JAKE "SULLY" SULLIVAN

STATS:
AGE: 14
TEAM: TITANS

BIO: The Titans are forming a track team for the first time, and Sully has taken it upon himself to convince the school's most talented teens to join up. There's just one problem — Sully didn't actually ask his friends Chris, Dwight, and Brett for permission before he volunteered them! Now, Sully must convince his hesitant friends to remain on the team, AND turn them into talented track stars...

Sports Illustrated KIDS

UP NEXT: *TRACK TEAM TITANS*

JAX AND FLYNN ROGERS

AGES: 15
TEAM: GOLIATHS

BIO: Jax and Flynn refer to themselves as "evil twins" mostly because they like to play pranks on everyone. When the Rogers twins are around, no one is safe from their gags.

BLZ vs BHS	3-1
TGR vs ROR	33-37
EAG vs BAN	14-7
SPA vs WLD	4-3
BAN vs ROR	21-15
ROR vs LIG	4-1
BLZ vs BHS	

CHRIS LANDRY

AGE: 14   **TEAM:** TITANS
BIO: Chris is the school's best football player. He's known as a touchdown-tossing quarterback who thrives under pressure.

CHRIS

DWIGHT REYNOLDS

AGE: 14   **TEAM:** TITANS
BIO: Dwight can outjump anybody on the court. At 14, he can already leap and reach the basketball rim.

DWIGHT

BRETT PULASKI

AGE: 14   **TEAM:** TITANS
BIO: Brett is the school's best baseball player. He's known as a speedy baserunner who never backs down.

BRETT

PRESENTS

TRACK TEAM
TITANS

A PRODUCTION OF

STONE ARCH BOOKS
a capstone imprint

written by *Stephanie True Peters*
illustrated by *Jesus Aburto*
inked by *Andres Esparza*
colored by *Fernando Cano*

designed and directed by Bob Lentz
edited by Sean Tulien
creative direction by Heather Kindseth
editorial management by Donald Lemke
editorial direction by Michael Dahl

Sports Illustrated KIDS *Track Team Titans* is published by Stone Arch Books,
151 Good Counsel Drive, P.O. Box 669, Mankato, Minnesota 56002.
www.capstonepub.com

Printed in the United States of America in Stevens Point, Wisconsin.
010319R

Summary: Track season is about to begin, and Sully is ready and raring
to run. But on the first day of tryouts, no other students show up! If the
Titans don't get more members, there won't be a track team. So Sully pays
a visit to the other sports teams, hoping their star athletes will join. None
of the other athletes think much of track and field. Sully will have to beat
them at their own sports to change their minds . . .

Library of Congress Cataloging-in-Publication Data
Peters, Stephanie True, 1965-
   Track team titans / written by Stephanie True Peters ; illustrated by
Aburtov, Andres Esparza, and Fares Maese.
      p. cm. -- (Sports Illustrated kids graphic novels)
   ISBN 978-1-4342-2224-4 (library binding) -- ISBN 978-1-4342-3072-0 (pbk.)
   1. Graphic novels. [1. Graphic novels. 2. Track and field--Fiction. 3.
Athletes--Fiction.] I. Aburto, Jesus, ill. II. Esparza, Andres, ill. III. Maese,
Fares, ill. IV. Title.
   PZ7.7.P44Tr 2011
   741.5'973--dc22   2010032922

Instead, they just ended up becoming my competition.

I'm looking forward to leaving you fools in the dust this year.

Yeah, you Titans are a big joke!

We'll see about that.

Thanks to us, the Goliaths were the track and field champs last year.

And we will be again this year, too!

You beat us? Wanna bet?

Bet what?

Bragging rights. Plus something extra...

Extra...?

If we win, you two have to shave your heads!

And when our team wins?

We'll all shave ours!

You've got a bet!

Say what?

Hey, Sully, wait a sec —

I'm outta here.

Looks like your track teammmates are already running, Sully!

Yeah — running away! Hahaha!

25

Dwight tried the hurdles.

CLANK!

Ooof!

Not bad, Brett!

But flatten out your trailing foot so the toe doesn't clip the bar.

Brett tested out the javelin.

Next time, aim higher up, not straight out.

So it travels more like a home run, not a line drive?

Exactly!

Chris puzzled over the shot put.

Nope! You put — or push — it away.

I have to throw this bowling ball?!

I told them everything.

Moments later, the relay was called.

Dwight got in the blocks and waited for the starting gun.

At the start of the final leg...

Get ready for the barber chair, Sully!

You sure about that...

...Jax?

BANG!

NOW!!!

41

Now it all rested on my shoulders...

TRACK TEAM TITANS OUTRUN ROGERS TWINS TO SEAL WIN!

RK
CK/FIELD

NT
ALL

3L
ALL

GL
ALL

3L
DBALL

BY THE NUMBERS

FINAL RANKINGS:
1ST PLACE: TITANS
2ND PLACE: GOLIATHS
3RD PLACE: BADGERS

STORY: The Titans got the better of the Goliaths as they rallied from behind to take home first place. Jax and Flynn Rogers both had their share of success, but ultimately their dishonesty cost them a shot at gold. Sully was quoted as saying, "I knew the twins were trying to pull a fast one on us, but we were still quicker!"

SZ POSTGAME *EXTRA*

WHERE *YOU* ANALYZE THE GAME!

Track and Field fans got a real treat today when the Titans faced off against the Goliaths. Let's go into the stands and ask some fans for their opinions on the day's track events . . .

DISCUSSION QUESTION 1

Which team name do you like better — the Titans or the Goliaths? If you had to pick a name for your school's team, what would you choose? Why?

DISCUSSION QUESTION 2

If you were on the Titans track team, which event would you choose to participate in? What skills do you have that would make you good at it? Talk about it.

WRITING PROMPT 1

Jax and Flynn cheated. Have you ever cheated at something? If not, do you know someone who has cheated? Write about your cheating experience.

WRITING PROMPT 2

Sully manages to convince his friends to try out for the track team. Talk about a time when you convinced someone else to do what you wanted.

INFO CENTER

GLOSSARY

COMPETITION (kom-puh-TISH-uhn)—rivalry offered by an opponent

CONDITION (kuhn-DISH-uhn)—something that is needed before another thing can happen

CONVINCE (kuhn-VINSS)—make someone believe you

CORNERED (KOR-nurd)—got someone into a position that traps them

DISQUALIFY (diss-KWOL-uh-fye)—prevent someone from taking part in an activity

PESTER (PESS-tur)—to keep annoying other people, often asking them something over and over again

SATISFYING (SAT-iss-fye-ing)—if something is satisfying, it makes you feel good or contented

SWARM (SWORM)—gather and move in large numbers, or surround and overwhelm in large numbers

VOLUNTEER (vol-uhn-TEER)—offfer to do something, often for free

EATORS

Stephanie True Peters › Author
After working more than 10 years as a children's book editor, Stephanie True Peters started writing books herself. She has since written 40 books, including the *New York Times* bestseller *A Princess Primer: A Fairy Godmother's Guide to Being a Princess*. When not at her computer, Peters enjoys playing with her two children, hitting the gym, or working on home improvement projects with her patient and supportive husband, Daniel.

Aburtov › Illustrator
Aburtov has worked in the comic book industry for more than 11 years. In that time, he has illustrated popular characters like Wolverine, Iron Man, Blade, and the Punisher. Recently, Aburtov started his own illustration studio called Graphikslava. He lives in Monterrey, Mexico, with his daughter, Ilka, and his beloved wife. Aburtov enjoys spending his spare time with family and friends.

Fares Maese › Inker
Fares Maese is a graphic designer and illustrator. He has worked as a colorist for Marvel Comics, and as a concept artist for the card and role-playing games *Pathfinder* and *Warhammer*. Fares loves spending time playing video games with his Graphikslava comrades, and he's an awesome drum player.

Fernando Cano › Colorist
Fernando Cano is an emerging illustrator born in Mexico City, Mexico. He currently resides in Monterrey, Mexico, where he works as a full-time illustrator and colorist at Graphikslava studio. He has done illustration work for Marvel, DC Comics, and role-playing games like *Pathfinder* from Paizo Publishing. In his spare time, he enjoys hanging out with friends, singing, rowing, and drawing!

LUKE LAWLESS IN:
BMX BLITZ

STONE ARCH BOOKS
a capstone imprint